Text by Marit Larsen
Illustrations by Jenny Løvlie
Text and illustrations copyright © 2019 by CAPPELEN DAMM AS. Oslo
Translation copyright © 2021 by Kari Dickson

Previously published as *Der Agnes Bor* by Cappelen Damm in Norway in 2019. Translated from Norwegian by Kari Dickson. First published in English by Amazon Crossing Kids in collaboration with Amazon Crossing in 2021.

Published by Amazon Crossing Kids, New York, in collaboration with Amazon Crossing

www.apub.com

Amazon, Amazon Crossing, and all related logos are trademarks of Amazon.com, Inc., or its affiliates.

ISBN-13: 9781542026758 (hardcover)
ISBN-10: 154202675X (hardcover)

The illustrations were rendered in digital media.

Book design by Tanya Ross-Hughes
Printed in China

First Edition

10 9 8 7 6 5 4 3 2 1

Agnes's Place

By Marit Larsen

Illustrations by Jenny Løvlie

Translated by Kari Dickson

amazon crossing kids

This city has so many buildings.

So many roofs
and walls
and doors

and windows
and doorbells
and trees

and secrets.

And this is where Agnes lives. Right here.
It is almost impossible to imagine that she would live anywhere else.

She knows she is at home before she even opens her eyes in the morning.

She knows who is baking, who is playing, and who is saying shush.

She knows that the birds are hungry and that she is the only one who remembers.

She knows who has the best parties,
who celebrates Christmas all year round,
and who gets the giggles when
they're all alone.

She knows who is outdoors and indoors,
and who never goes out at all.

She knows what it is like to be the only child
in a place full of adults who never have time.

From her window on the third floor Agnes looks down at a perfect puddle that is just the right size when it rains just enough.

The new girl was standing beside it when Agnes
saw her for the first time.

The girl's gaze moved slowly up the wall.
What was she looking for?
Is she looking for me? Agnes thought.

That was before Agnes knew that Anna was Anna.

Agnes squeezed her eyes shut
and opened them again,
but the girl was still there.

Did she have a key?
Was she going to live here?

Agnes looked through the little peephole in the door that made her invisible, her nose pressed to the cold metal. The new girl stole silently past Amadeus, who was lying curled up, pretending to sleep. Agnes giggled without a sound.

Box after box after box
passed by Agnes's door on their way up
to the fifth floor.

Agnes had an idea. She got a large piece of paper and drew the tree in the backyard with the two empty swings. She drew the tracks left in the gravel by those who had jumped off.

Then she wrote

in big letters.

Agnes waited until all was quiet,
then crept out
and sneaked up the stairs,

and slipped the drawing
through the letter box.

She felt her heart pounding
in her cheeks and ears.
"Done," she whispered to Amadeus.

Playing alone on the swing is very different from playing alone on the swing
when you are waiting for someone who does not show up.

The next day everything was as usual when Agnes woke up.
Only everything was different.

She crept out of bed, opened her window wide,
and put a handful of birdseed in the birdhouse.
Then another. And another.
Nothing.

Swooooosh!

Five, fifteen, maybe fifty birds flew up in a flock,
right past Agnes's window and up toward
the roof.

They settled outside the new girl's window.
Agnes caught a glimpse of her arm
on the windowsill.

After breakfast
Agnes went down to the swings again
and practiced some tricks—some new,
some old, and some wild and wonderful.

Every so often she would look up at her building,
which was somehow a new place now.

Suddenly everything Agnes usually did was all about the new girl.

Did she see what Agnes saw?

Did she hear what Agnes heard?

Agnes waited by the swings each day. She waited until she got hungry
or it was so late that her mom called her in.

Meanwhile, the new girl
had discovered the puddle all on her own.

She held concerts for anyone that would listen.
She did lots of fun things.

It almost seemed
as if the only thing Anna was not interested in
was Agnes.

Even Amadeus had found a new playmate.

Disappointed, Agnes went down to get Emilia's newspaper,
just as she had always done. Agnes knew exactly which stone
made her tall enough to reach into the mailbox. But today it was empty.
The newspaper was not there.

"It is a bit strange, isn't it, that you can just move into a place without asking everyone who lives there if they think it's okay?" Agnes said in a quiet voice.

"Well, now—we've all been new at one time or another. Even me.
That's a really strange thought for you perhaps?"
There weren't many teeth left in Emilia's grin. "Now, would you like a waffle?"

But Agnes didn't want one. A waffle is not much comfort when you are five
and have no secrets left to share.

Then suddenly there they were on the stairs. Both of them, in the same moment.

And they were both the same size.
And they were both just as quiet.

Agnes looked at Anna's hat.
Anna looked at Agnes's sweater.

They could have been knit from the same ball of wool.

Anna held out her hand and opened it. Agnes thought it looked like
she had the whole universe in the palm of her hand.

Before they knew it, the stairwell had transformed into
an ocean of blue, green, turquoise, yellow, purple, and red waves,
and Agnes and Anna stared at the waves
and each other,
and then Agnes started to laugh,
which made Anna laugh too,
and they stood there with their mouths open wide,
laughing, louder and louder, on the seabed,
until Anna carefully gathered up all her marbles in one hand
and grabbed Agnes's hand with the other.

A door became a stair became a long ladder to a place
where Agnes had never been before.

It turned out that Anna had her own secrets.
And they were wild and wonderful.